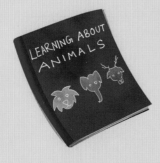

Dedicated to my parents, husband, and family. This book is also dedicated to my son, Kingston, and my students, for renewing my love of books.

Boys Unboxed and the distinctive Boys Unboxed logo are trademarks of PHraseD, Jr., LLC.

Text and illustration © 2021 by PHraseD, Jr. LLC
Illustrations by Fx and Color Studio

978-1-7375460-0-9 (Hardcover)
978-1-7375460-1-6 (Paperback)
978-1-7375460-2-3 (E-book)

Printed and bound in China

For information about custom editions, special sales and premium and corporate purchases, or to request permissions for use, please contact PHraseD, Jr. LLC at phrasedllc@gmail.com

https://www.phrasedllc.com/phrased-jr

I LOVE A
GOOD BOOK

Dr. Kimberlie Harris
Illustrated by Fx And Color Studio

I love a good book, a good book with my daddy,
after a bath, when I'm almost ready for bed.

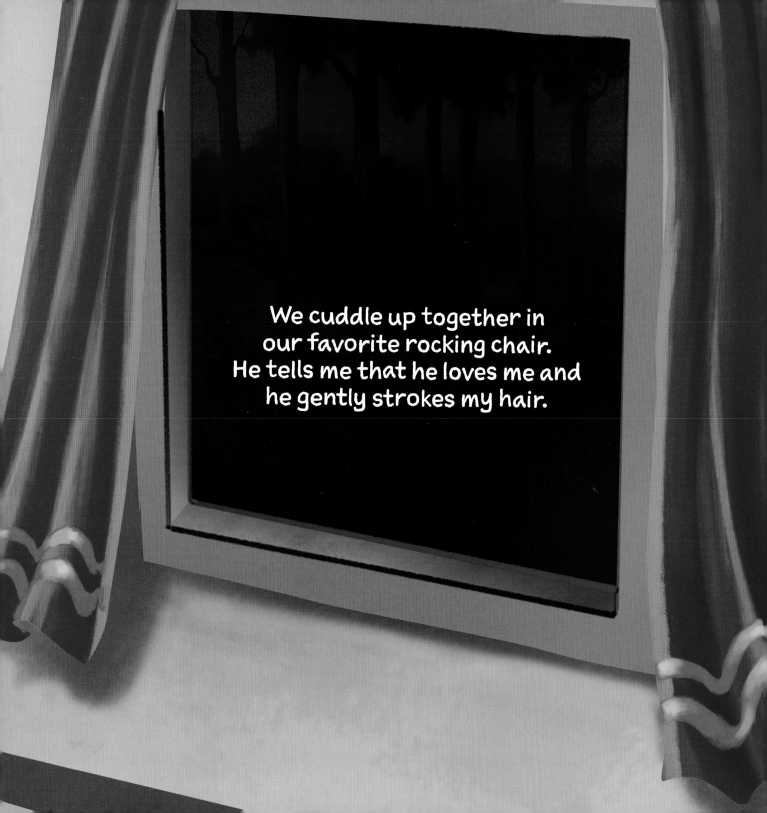

We cuddle up together in
our favorite rocking chair.
He tells me that he loves me and
he gently strokes my hair.

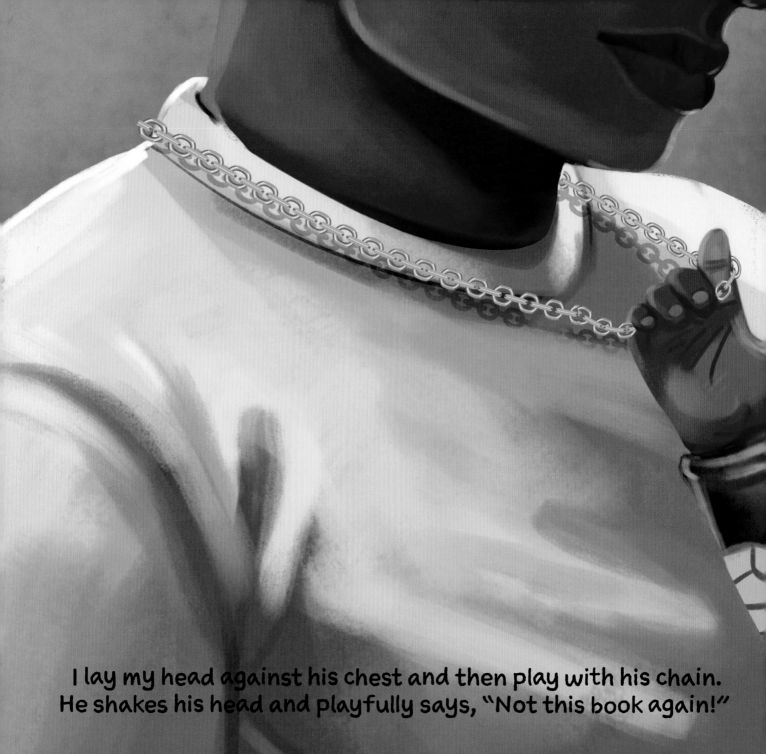

I lay my head against his chest and then play with his chain.
He shakes his head and playfully says, "Not this book again!"

My dad makes funny faces and makes even better voices.
We're a super team, since I make all the best book choices.

I love a good book,
a good book with my daddy.

I love a good book,
a good book with my mommy,
in the middle of the day,
right before my nap.

We always read together on a blanket on the floor.
She reads some in a language that I've never heard before.

She cuddles me and kisses me between each of the lines.
I try hard to act like I'm so mad, but I don't really mind.

My job is to turn the pages until we are done.
I always beg my mom to reread each and every one.

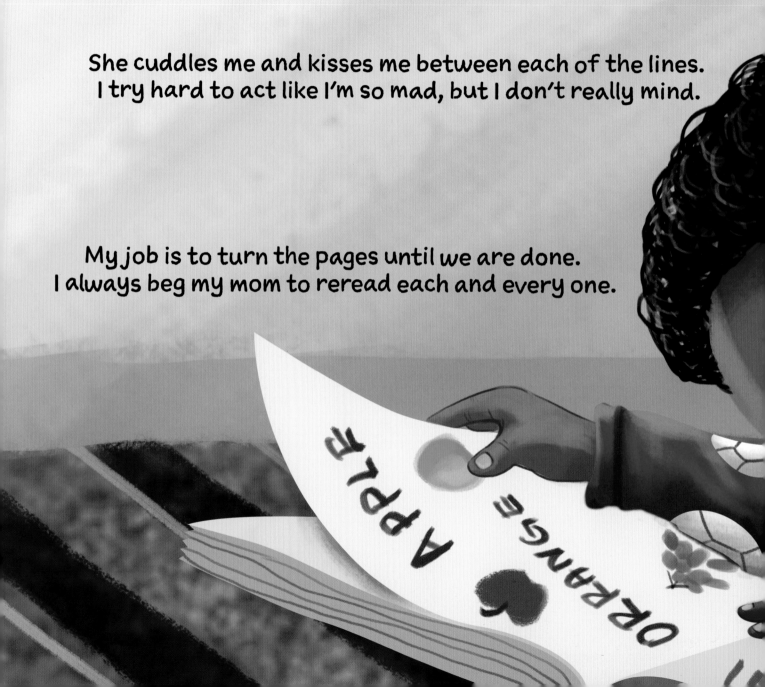

I love a good book,
a good book with my mommy.

I love a good book,
a good book with my Granna,
early in the morning,
before the sun is high.

I sit and wait for Granna on the couch or in my seat.
She fixes me delicious and nutritious snacks to eat.

My Granna picks cool books to read that teach me something new,
like numbers, colors, words, shapes, animals and objects, too.

When we're finished reading, Granna tells me I'm so cute.
It always makes me smile because it's the honest truth.

I love a good book,
a good book with
my Granna.

I love a good book, a good book with my book bud.
She is a librarian and knows about books.

BUBBLES

We go to see her after breakfast, once I eat my food.
I love each of our library trips. They always help my mood.

We read then practice signing, and I show off what I know.
Sometimes there's a craft to do or some big puppet show.

My favorite part is getting treats for books I read at home.
The best reward's a token for a tasty ice-cream cone.

I love a good book,
a good book with my book bud.

I love a good book, a good book when I'm alone,
when no one is there to bother
me or get in my way.

I pick out a good one and then check the coast is clear.
I listen very carefully for noises coming near.

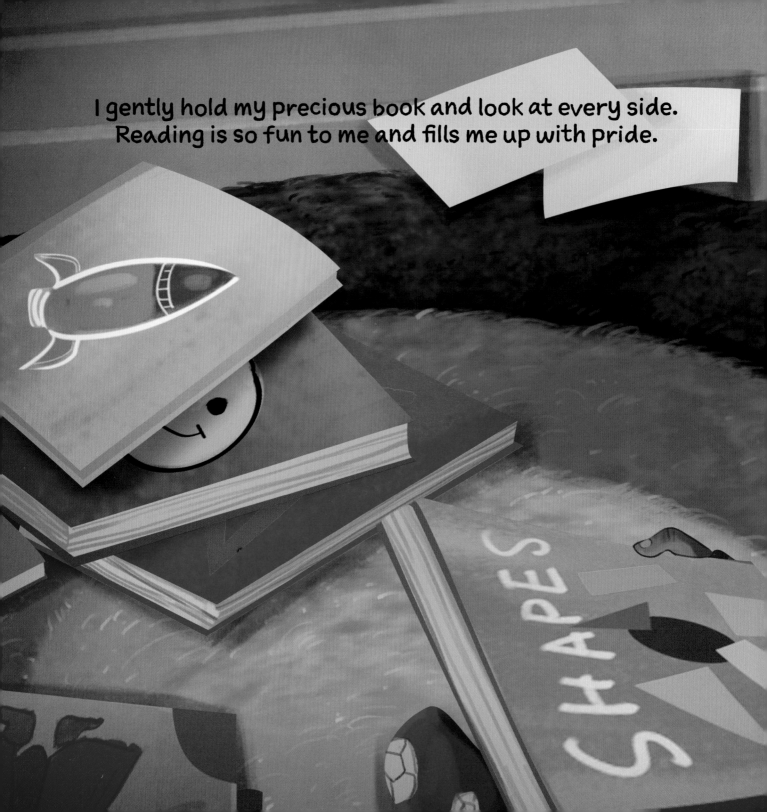

I gently hold my precious book and look at every side.
Reading is so fun to me and fills me up with pride.

Every moment with a book is such a cherished gift.
Reading makes me happy and it gives my heart a lift.

I love a good book,
when it's clenched between my teeth.

I love a good book,
a good book that I can eat.

Look out for the next book in the Boys Unboxed series:
WONDOGFILLED

Dr. Kimberlie Harris is a teacher, mom, blogger, and freelance writer turned author. She was born and raised in Kingston, Jamaica, but now resides with her husband and son in Georgia, U.S.A. Dr. Harris enjoys helping children learn to read and love books, be curious about their surroundings, and use that curiosity to conquer their world.

I Love a Good Book is the first book in the Boys Unboxed series. Dr. Harris wrote I Love a Good Book and the other titles in the Boys Unboxed series to inspire young boys to read.

Dr. Harris has worked to improve learning outcomes for children, especially in reading and writing, for 17 years. She has a PhD. in curriculum and instruction, a masters in early childhood education and dual bachelor of arts degrees in English and Spanish.

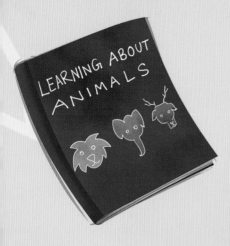

LEARNING ABOUT
ANIMALS

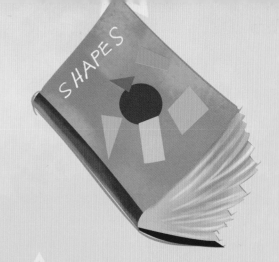

SHAPES

SHAPES

My Big
Book on
Jamaica

Mi Gran Libro
Sobre Jamaica

I LOVE A
GOOD BOOK

BUBBLES